When my friends ask me why my wife and I are so into our kids hockey "careers," I often tell them, "Imagine you have front row season tickets to your favorite team, and after each game you get to have lunch and hang out with your favorite player!" (Author unknown)

– Richard Torrey

Kane Miller, A Division of EDC Publishing

Text and illustrations copyright © Richard Torrey 2011

For information contact:
Kane Miller, A Division of EDC Publishing
PO Box 470663
Tulsa, OK 74147-0663
www.kanemiller.com
www.edcpub.com
www.usbornebooksandmore.com

Library of Congress Control Number: 2010943437

Manufactured by Regent Publishing Services, Hong Kong
Printed March 2014 in ShenZhen, Guangdong, China

2 3 4 5 6 7 8 9 10

ISBN: 978-1-61067-053-1

A HOCKEY Story

By Richard Torrey

Whack!

Kane Miller
A DIVISION OF EDC PUBLISHING

Every Saturday morning I wake up really, really early and go to the ice rink.

It's my favorite place because it's where I play my favorite sport – hockey. But today is even more special. Today I'm playing on a new team!

What if I don't know anybody on my team?

What if I fall down or something?

What if I forget how to play?

When I get there I always have to look at the ice for a minute.
It's smooth and cold. It's white and bright.
I think about skating out there with my new team.
My tummy starts to feel funny.

It's time to get dressed. My hockey bag is big, but it has wheels so I can pull it all by myself. What's inside? Everything I need so I won't get hurt if I fall, or bump into someone on the ice.

What if everyone is better than me?

What if my new coach is mean?

What if no one talks to me?

What if I have to go to the bathroom?

My stomach hurts.

I put on my shoulder pads, my elbow pads, my hockey pants, my shin pads, and my gloves – they're my favorite!

Next I put on my new jersey. It's yellow and red – my two favorite colors.

It has a bear on the front. (My new team's name is the Bears.) And it has my number on the back – 76 – the best number in the whole world!

When I put it on it feels special.
I wish I could wear my new jersey every day.

My most favorite things are my skates. They're sharp and shiny and new, and I don't even need help putting them on! But my mom and dad always take turns tying them tight so I can skate my fastest.

Now it's time to show my new teammates what a good hockey player I am!

My new teammates and I skate around the ice together.

We practice our passing...

... and we practice our shooting.

My new coach's name is Charlie. He's really nice, and he has a moustache. He's a good skater, too!

Before the game, Coach Charlie has all the Bears bunch up together. He says if we always try our hardest, we'll get better every time we play. But mostly he tells us to have fun.

And we do!

... is going out for breakfast after the game!